**Pepper the Porcupine and the Big Parade**
Written by Jourdan Lewanda and Illustrated by Andrew Latona
Text and illustrations copyright © 2013 by B'nai B'rith International
ISBN: 978-0-578-12409-4

Published as part of the *Diverse Minds Youth Writing Challenge* by:

B'NAI B'RITH INTERNATIONAL

2020 K Street NW, 7th Floor
Washington, DC 20006
202-857-6600
www.bnaibrith.org

# Pepper
## the
# Porcupine
# And the Big Parade!

Written by:
Jourdan Lewanda

Illustrated by:
Andrew Latona

On a sunny spring morning
When the birds were all singing
Young Pepper awoke
To the telephone ringing...

"AUDITIONS TODAY!"
The voice proudly exclaimed
"TO BE IN THE TOWN'S
SPRING MUSIC PARADE."

Young Pepper had dreamed
For years upon years
Of playing a song
Alongside of his peers.

But then Pepper remembered
A fact he'd forgotten:
He was no good at music—
In fact, he was rotten!

So he decided right then
To ask his friend Blake,
The kindly old bobcat
To teach him the bass.

He found his old friend
Standing under a tree-
Playing his music
As smooth as could be.

"May I try?" Pepper asked,
To which the cat said,
"You can try little buddy,
But it's over your head."

Then Pepper looked up
And saw Blake was right,
He'd need to find something
That suited his height.

So on Pepper went
To find something little,
And came across Franny Fox
Playing her fiddle.

"How perfect!" he thought,
For Franny was small,
"I won't have to worry
About not being tall!"

He reached for the fiddle
(After asking politely)

But trying to play it
Didn't work out so nicely...

The quills on his coat
Made it harder to play,
When he reached for the notes
All the strings broke away.

"I'm so sorry" cried Pepper
(His head hanging low)
"I don't think I'll *ever*
Fit in with the show."

So Pepper moved on
Not wanting to quit,
And found Tyrone T-Rex
Wailing on his trumpet!

"Something small I won't break!"
Pepper shouted with glee,
Oh how I do hope
Tyrone will teach me.

So Pepper approached
His dinosaur friend,
Who then gladly agreed
To lend Pepper a hand.

Tyrone then told Pepper
The thing he should do:
Just blow in the mouthpiece
And let music play through!

So Pepper blew out
As much air as he could,
But the sound didn't come out
The way that it should!

It squawked and it squeaked,
(It sounded quite bad)
Pepper failed once again
And it made him feel sad...

At home Pepper wondered
What else he could try,
He had no ideas
So he started to cry.

He was short, he was sharp,
He was everything wrong–
There would be no way on Earth
He could join in the song!

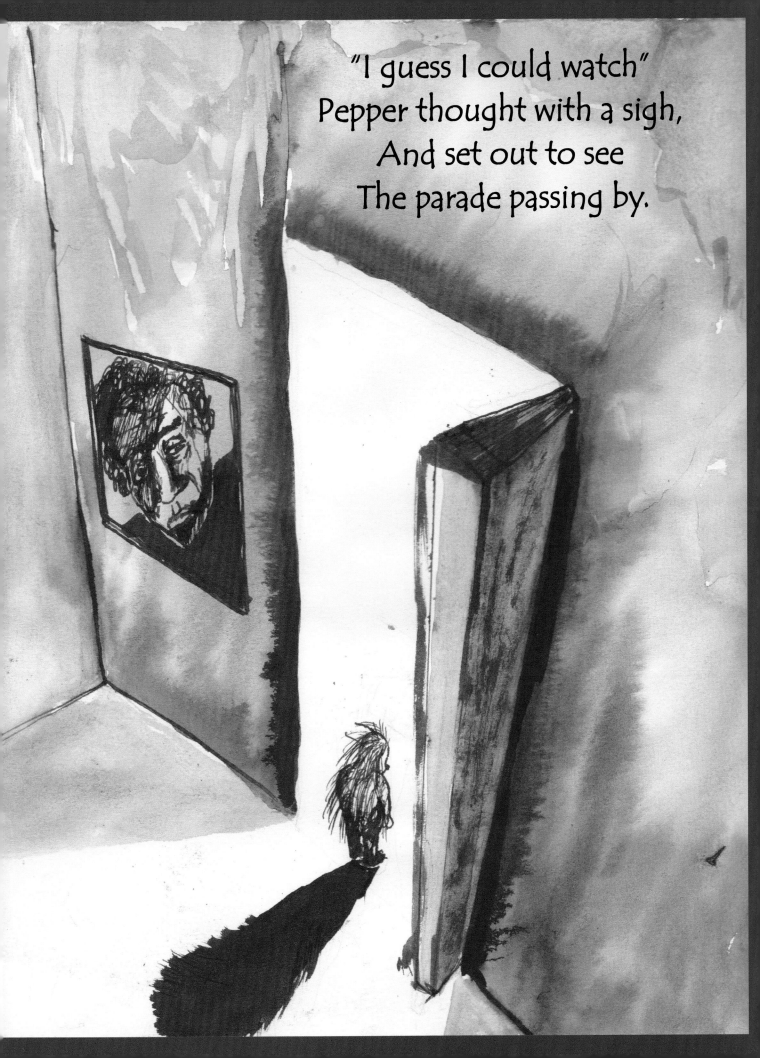

"I guess I could watch"
Pepper thought with a sigh,
And set out to see
The parade passing by.

As he got to the place
Where his friends were all playing,
His feet started moving-
The sight was amazing!

Pepper couldn't play trumpet,
Or fiddle or bass,
But what he *could* do
Was dance with great grace!

"What a wonderful dancer!"
The director exclaimed.
"You there, young man–
Will you lead our parade?"

Pepper couldn't believe
What he heard to be true,
"But I can't play an instrument
I don't fit in with you."

"I'm too different to be
In the parade with my friends,
They all have such talent-
I couldn't lead them."

The director just smiled
At Pepper and then
Said the most wonderful words
That have ever been said:

"It's not wrong to be different–
In fact look around–
All these creatures are special
No duplicates found!

"We have trumpets and fiddles,
And oboes and flutes,
But what we need most
Is you leading our group.

"Your rhythm and style
Could never be beat
You do what you're best at
While moving your feet.

"And without a conductor
Our band falls apart
So what do you say, boy?
The parade's about to start!"

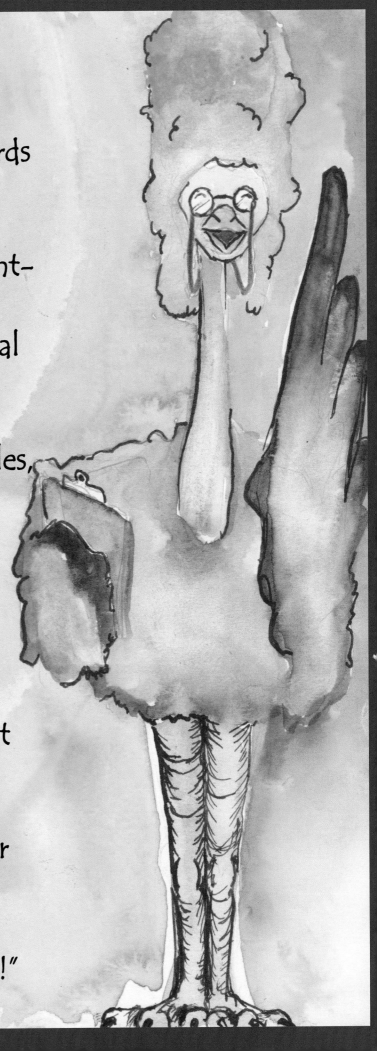

Pepper smiled excitedly
Then took the baton
And with a deep breath,
Started dancing along.

Pepper led the parade
For block after block
As the band played the music,
From Classical to rock.

When the band was all done,
Creatures cheered and they clapped,
For never before
Had the parade gone like that.

It was the best it had been
In the history of the land
Thanks to Pepper the Porcupine
Leading the band.

B'nai B'rith International

*Diverse Minds Youth Writing Challenge*

**Pepper the Porcupine and the Big Parade**, written by Jourdan Lewanda and illustrated by Andrew Latona was created as part of the B'nai B'rith International *Diverse Minds Youth Writing Challenge* in the Washington, D.C metro area.

The *Diverse Minds Youth Writing Challenge* is an education and awareness initiative created by B'nai B'rith International as part of its series of programs developed to combat bigotry through the promotion of tolerance and equality. The contest aims to present positive views about diversity to a broad range of youth in order to achieve tolerance within our communities.

Executed through public and private high schools within the Washington, D.C. metro area, the contest asks high school students to write and illustrate a children's book that tells a story of diversity and tolerance. Participants are required to think about how these principles can improve our world, and then create innovative ways to teach these ideas to children through the creation of a book.

Book submissions were reviewed by a judging panel comprised of business leaders, educators, non-profit community leaders and local officials. Scholarship prizes in the amounts of $5,000, $2,000 and $1,000 are awarded to the first, second and third place winners, and the first-place winning book is professionally published and donated to elementary schools, libraries and literacy organizations within the District of Columbia and surrounding areas.

For more information about the program and next year's contest, please visit www.bnaibrith.org/diverseminds.

# Pepper the Porcupine and the Big Parade

**Written by**
Jourdan Lewanda

**Illustrated by**
Andrew Latona

**James Hubert Blake High School**
Silver Spring, MD

**Teacher:** Ms. Amy Branson
**Principal:** Mr. Christopher Berry

Jourdan Lewanda is a graduating senior at James Hubert Blake High School. She has earned awards such as an AP Scholar with Distinction through the College Board, as well as awards for her work as an actress, including the Superintendent's Award for Theatre and the Award of Excellence in the Arts through the National Society of Arts and Letters and the Kennedy Center, among others. When she begins college in the fall, she hopes to pursue musical theatre or acting, along with a minor in English.

Andrew Latona is also a graduating senior at James Hubert Blake High School, where he has excelled in AP English, Art, and Music classes and serves as a captain of the Swim Team. He is also the leader of the Eubie Blake Jazz Quintet, and he recently won the Mid Atlantic Jazz Festival art competition. He has always enjoyed drawing and painting, and hopes to continue pursuing his passions throughout his lifetime.

## SECOND PLACE WINNER

### BIRD IN BLUES
**Written and Illustrated by**

David Ng
and
Kayla Trinh

Damascus High School

## THIRD PLACE WINNER

### EVERYONE IS ROYAL
**Written and Illustrated by**

Chala A. M. Tshitundu
and
Rebecca H. Hamilton-Levi

Montgomery Blair High School

# Diverse Minds Youth Writing Challenge
# WASHINGTON, D.C. METRO AREA
# JUDGING PANEL

B'nai B'rith International would like to thank the following judging panel members for donating their time and talents to reviewing the finalists' submissions and selecting the winners for the 2013 *Diverse Minds Youth Writing Challenge.*

**Alexander D. Baumgarten**
*Director of Government Relations*
The Episcopal Church

**Ari Z. Brooks**
*Executive Director*
Friends of the Library, Montgomery County

**Donna Cooper**
*Region Vice President*
Pepco

**Thomas Graham**
*Region President*
Pepco

**Vincent C. Gray**
*Mayor*
District of Columbia

**Dr. Sybille A. Jagusch**
*Chief, Children's Literature Center*
Library of Congress

**Daniel S. Mariaschin**
*Executive Vice President*
B'nai B'rith International

**Kenneth Parker O'Neil**
*Senior Vice President*
Pepco Holdings Inc.

**Dr. DeRionne P. Pollard**
*President*
Montgomery College

**Joseph Rigby**
*Chairman of the Board, President, and Chief Executive Officer*
Pepco Holdings Inc.

**Judy Sierra**
*Children's Author, Poet and Folklorist*

**Ingird M. Turner, Esq.**
*Council Member 4th District*
Prince George's County, MD

**Jim Vance**
*News Anchor*
WRC-TV

**Dave Velasquez**
*Executive Vice President*
Pepco Holdings Inc.

# PROGRAM SUPPORTER

## A PHI Company

**B'nai B'rith International would like to thank PEPCO for their support of the *Diverse Minds Youth Writing Challenge* in the Washington, D.C. Metro Area.**

Pepco has been providing reliable electric service for more than one hundred years. Today, we work around the clock to deliver electricity to more than 793,000 customers in Maryland and the District of Columbia. We're proud of the accolades we've earned for service, reliability and customer satisfaction.

We also place a high value on being a good corporate citizen. We conduct our business responsibly and in a manner designed to protect the health and safety of our employees, our customers, the general public and the environment. We encourage and support our employees who give their time and energy creating a brighter future for others, and we are fortunate to serve an area so rich in diversity.

That's why Pepco attaches great importance to learning from and working with the diverse cultures that make up our community in the District of Columbia and Montgomery and Prince George's counties in Maryland.